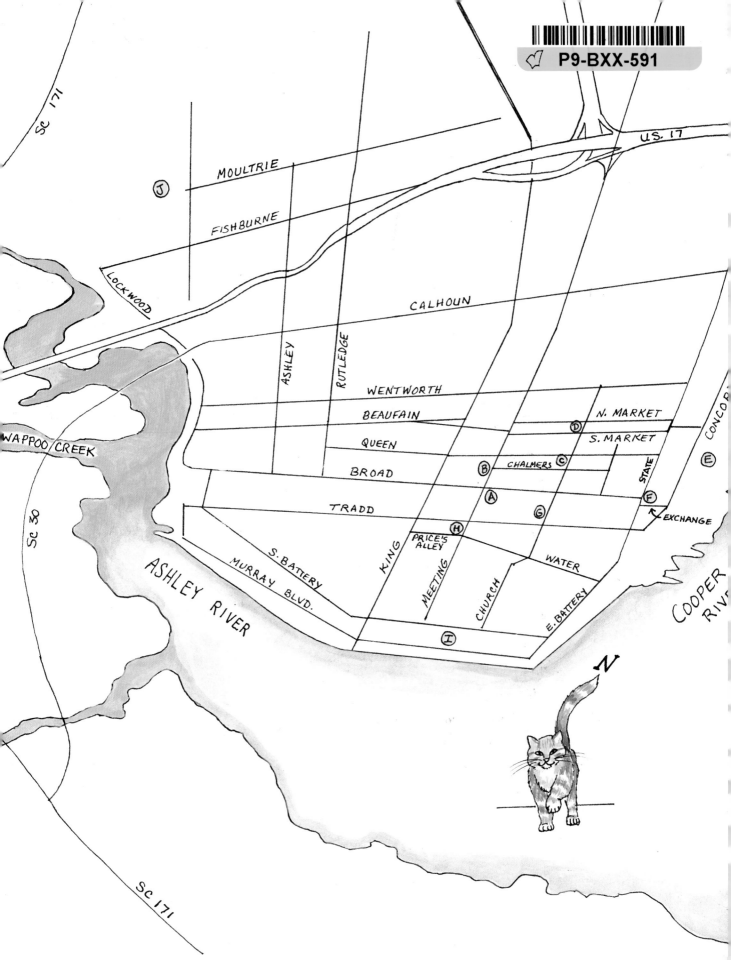

Published by Sandlapper Publishing Co., Inc.
Orangeburg, South Carolina 29115

Printed in Hong Kong

Library of Congress Cataloging-in-Publication Data

Chappell, Ruth Paterson.
    The mysterious tail of a Charleston cat : a tour guide for
children of all ages / by Ruth Paterson Chappell and Bess Paterson
Shipe ; with illustrations by Dean Wroth.
       p. cm.
    Summary: While keeping an eye out for a missing cat, four cousins
explore the city of Charleston, South Carolina.
   ISBN 0-87844-130-1
   [1. Charleston (S.C.)—Fiction. 2. Cats—Fiction. 3. Lost and
found possessions—Fiction. 4. Cousins—Fiction.]   I. Shipe, Bess
Paterson. II. Wroth, Dean, ill. III. Title.
PZ7.C37285My   1996
[Fic]—dc20   96-26065
                                    CIP
                                     AC

dedicated with love
to our
present and future
grandchildren

Map Key

DAY 1

DAY 2

The Beginning

"Wait, we can't start the tour yet. I can't find Silas." Chad sounded worried.

Our little family tour group came to a stop on the Tradd Street sidewalk.

"I told you to put the cat inside an hour ago," Uncle Jim said.

"I couldn't find him then, Dad. You know how he's always running off."

"We just can't lose him," Caroline declared. "He's a very lovable cat."

"When he wants to be," Uncle Jim teased, grinning.

"Come on, Dad. Just because he doesn't always come when we call him—" Chad began.

"He doesn't want us to think he comes because he *has* to," Caroline interrupted. "He likes to *surprise* us."

"He sure did surprise **me** last night," I said.

Chad and I looked at each other and laughed.

• • •

What happened was . . .

It was my first night in Charleston and I didn't know about Silas. Chad and I were on the floor, half in and half out of our sleeping bags, when all of a sudden, from out of nowhere, this big orange cat jumped to the floor beside us. I jumped too! He walked right across Chad and snuggled down next to me, sort of under my arm.

1

"Go away, cat."

"Don't you like cats?" Chad sounded surprised.

"*Well . . .*"

Just then, Silas started to purr. I didn't just hear him. I could actually **feel** him purring.

"He likes you," Chad said. "I guess he knows you're family."

Silas was all warm and furry and had obviously settled in for the night.

"Well—he can sleep here with me if he wants to." And he did.

• • •

"We'll just have to leave him outside," said Aunt Sue. "He'll be all right. I do believe that cat has nine lives!"

"Yes," Uncle Jim agreed. "He's a very athletic cat. Come on then, gang," he directed. "Let's go. We have to show Charleston to your California cousins."

And that's how this whole awesome adventure began.

We Start Our Walking Tour

My name is David Blake. I was almost eleven that spring. My sister, Emmy, was seven. Our parents had always wanted to take us to visit the house where Dad and his brother, Uncle Jim, had grown up—the house in which the Charleston Blakes still lived.

So that you can keep us straight, let me introduce the family. Aunt Sue and Uncle Jim and our cousins, Caroline and Chad, are the Charleston Blakes. Chad was almost eleven, like me. Caroline was twelve. My mom and dad are Mary and Allan Blake, and they have Emmy and me.

Emmy and I were excited about meeting our cousins. We were excited about everything! Charleston was very different from La Jolla, California, where we live.

The house on Tradd Street was long and narrow. It's called a *single house* because it's only one-room wide. The front door is on the side of the house, which faces the street, and it opens onto a porch, called a piazza, that runs the full length of the house. Aunt Sue said that was because long ago, before air conditioning, Charleston houses were built so the cool ocean breezes could blow straight through in the summertime.

"I'm glad you all have on your walking shoes," Uncle Jim said as we started out.

Emmy was skipping ahead, trying to keep up with Caroline.

"Why does Charleston look like it's long ago *now*?" we all heard her ask. Everybody laughed, but it did sort of look like we had stepped back in time.

The streets were narrow and lined with old houses. Some of them had gardens with walls around them. A horse pulling a carriage full of tourists clippity-clopped past us as we walked along. Some of the carriage's passengers smiled and waved to us.

"Charming. Charming," my mom kept saying.

"This is the historic district where lots of things are still the way they used to be when there weren't any cars and ladies wore hoop skirts," Caroline told us. She twirled around holding out her skirt, and Emmy did it too.

"Oh, yuk!" Chad groaned. He always knew when his sister was showing off.

Chad jumped up on one of the low garden walls and started walking along the top. I did it too.

"Be careful, children," my mom called after us.

"Don't worry about them," Dad said happily. "Jim and I used to walk for blocks on these old walls when we were kids."

Chad wasn't listening to the grown-ups. He was looking down at the wall.

He suddenly pointed and I looked down. In places where the long green vines weren't growing over the brick there was a trail of small, muddy paw prints.

"I think Silas has been walking on this wall," he said.

"How do you know it wasn't just any old cat?"

"Because there's something different about Silas. Most cats have four toes on each paw. Silas has five."

"Oh." I had to think about that.

"So," Chad said smiling, "maybe he's coming with us."

4

A.

The Four Corners of Law
and St. Michael's Church

"Step lively, now," Uncle Jim called. "We're going to walk down Meeting Street to Broad. That intersection is a famous place in Charleston. It's called the Four Corners of Law."

"Why?" asked Emmy.

Dad looked back and smiled. "Why do you think?"

By the time we reached the intersection I thought I had it figured out, but I looked carefully at the names on the buildings to make sure.

"Dad, I see law buildings on three of the corners: City Hall, the Charleston County Courthouse—"

"And the United States Court House and Post Office," Emmy chimed in. . . . It really wasn't fair though, because Caroline told her.

"Great! Each building represents a different branch of law," Dad said, "city, county, and national."

"And on the other corner," added Aunt Sue, "is Saint Michael's Church. That represents God's law."

As we walked across the street she continued, "Charleston has many beautiful old churches, but this is the oldest. If you children look up, you'll see that the clock in the tower has four faces, each one facing a different direction."

"The steeple's 186 feet high," Uncle Jim told us. "It was used as a lookout in the 1700s. From that height, the watchman could see friendly

5

ships sailing in or pirates about to attack."

"We'd better move along," Aunt Sue said. "We have a lot of places to go and something special in mind for the end of the day."

The grown-ups walked on, but Chad, Caroline, Emmy, and I just stood staring up, because something strange was happening.

The big minute hand on one of the clock's faces whizzed down from 12 to 6. There was a jumbled clatter of chimes, as if the quarter hour and the half hour were striking together.

"Upon my word!" We turned to see an old man, his camera slung over his shoulder, looking up. "Upon my word, I thought for a moment I saw some kind of creature hanging from that minute hand."

Along the top of the railing of the balcony above the clock, something was moving—something quick and slithery—something that flicked an orange tail and disappeared.

"Here, kitty. Here, kitty," Caroline called. She began to jump around, waving her hand toward the steeple. People on the street stared at her as they passed by—some looked as if they were thinking she was definitely weird.

"You know he never comes when you call him." Chad shook his head. "He only comes when he wants to."

I suddenly had an idea. "Of course, he's not my cat, but I think if he *was* my cat, I'd walk along and pretend I didn't know he was following. Then maybe he'd come close enough to catch."

"Let's try that," Chad said excitedly.

We all marched along the sidewalk with our eyes aimed straight ahead. . . . *Well, maybe I did sneak a look,* but I didn't see Silas.

B.
Hibernian Society Hall

"I do wish you'd stop worrying," Aunt Sue said as we caught up with our parents. "That cat is probably lying in the sunshine right now on the roof of our piazza."

My dad was paused on the sidewalk looking at a tall, black, iron gate. Dad's an architect, as well as somebody who grew up in Charleston, so I knew we were about to get a lecture—but I didn't really mind. Sometimes he makes us notice things that we would have gone right past, without ever seeing.

"Observe this wonderful old grillwork." *Observe* is a word my dad loves to use. "This is the gate of the Hibernian Society Hall. Look closely, kids. What kind of design do you see on that entrance gate?"

It was easy, so I let Emmy answer.

"A harp," she said proudly.

"Right." Dad went on, "It's an Irish harp. Hibernian means Irish. The harp represents music. This hall is where the great St. Cecilia balls have been held. St. Cecilia is the patron saint of music."

I expected to see Caroline start whirling around again, but she didn't.

"The detail on this old building is fascinating," Dad was saying. "Look up at the pediment."

"What's a pediment?" Emmy was always asking questions.

"The roof goes up in a triangle, like the roofs on some old Roman buildings. Why do you think that little imitation owl is up there, David?"

I looked up—way up.

8

"Gosh, I don't know."

"To scare away pigeons, son."

We all stood still, staring up. A flock of pigeons flushed suddenly from somewhere on the roof and took off as if they were shot into the sky. The little owl just sat there.

"Silas likes to chase pigeons," Chad said thoughtfully. "I think they'd be a lot more scared of Silas than they would of that little old owl."

"Could a cat climb all the way up there?" I asked.

The grown-ups were already walking on.

"Silas could," said Chad. "I bet he could."

"We simply have to catch him," Caroline said. "That's very dangerous, even for a cat."

C.

Dock Street Theatre

"This is Washington Park," Aunt Sue was saying to my mom as we caught up once again. "We'll cut through here to get to the Dock Street Theatre."

We kids were cool. We didn't say a word about Silas. We just kept walking.

Arriving at a very old sandstone building, Dad stopped to admire the arches and wrought iron balconies. Then we all went inside.

"We'll let Chad be our guide," Uncle Jim said. "He was in a production put on here by the young people's theater group last Christmas, so he knows all about this place."

"Well," Chad began, acting as if he really was a guide, "the first theater building in America stood right here. It was built long ago, in 1736. Later, the Planters' Hotel was built here, on the very same site. And then, much later, *this* theater was built inside those same old sort-of-crumbly walls. The *important* thing is it was made to look like a theater would have looked long ago."

"Very good," Aunt Sue praised.

"Please observe," Chad continued, trying to look dignified, and also trying not to laugh, "the boxes on either side of the theater. From there you can look down on the stage and have a special view. On the shield over the stage, the lion and unicorn are fighting."

While the others looked up at the boxes and the shield, I saw Chad staring at the stage curtain. It was billowing in and out at the bottom as if

11

something small was moving along behind.

Chad and I didn't have to say anything. He went to one side of the stage and I went to the other. We moved quietly along the curtain from each end until we met in the middle—and grabbed! But all we felt was each other's hands.

"What *are* you children doing?" my mom asked.

"Nothing," answered Chad sheepishly.

"Just fooling around," I added.

We felt pretty silly just then.

"I know what they were doing," Emmy said. "They were trying to catch Silas."

Little sisters are like that sometimes. . . .

Our moms just smiled at each other and shook their heads.

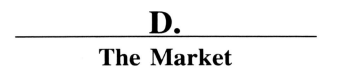

D.

The Market

"Now we'll walk right up Church Street to the Market." Uncle Jim guided us on.

When we got there, we California Blakes just stood and looked for a few minutes, trying to take it all in. Of course, we have markets in California too, but this Charleston market was different—I guess because it looked as if it had been there for such a long time. The red brick building at the front of the Market had tall arches that were open to the street so visitors could walk in and out. The whole place was filled with people bustling about, buying and selling things.

"You'll find all kinds of local crafts here," Aunt Sue told us.

"I want to find something typical of Charleston to take home to our neighbor," Mom was saying. My mom likes to shop, but I usually think shopping is boring.

We started walking through the aisles, between the stalls. It was noisy, with lots of talking and laughing. There was so much to look at, our parents kept stopping. There were stalls of vegetables and fruit and big bunches of bright flowers, as well as all the other things. My mom bought benne wafers and pralines.

There were good smells, too—some of them coming from the restaurants along Market Street.

I was getting hungry.

"When do we eat lunch?" I asked Chad, but he didn't seem to hear me. When Chad has something on his mind, it's hard to get his attention.

"This might be where we can catch Silas," he said. "There are so many things he could get into—or under. Maybe he'll stand still and won't know we're trying to creep up on him."

Caroline agreed. "He likes to poke into things. Chad, you and David take the right side of the aisle. Keep looking everywhere. Emmy and I'll take the left. If Silas is still coming with us, maybe we'll see him."

The grown-ups had stopped to watch the basket ladies weaving baskets out of long golden pieces of sweet grass. A crowd had gathered, looking on in amazement as the ladies' fingers moved so fast, creating different designs.

Suddenly Emmy darted away.

"Emmy!" Mom called, running after her.

I ran too. I had seen Emmy inching along, through the crowd, looking toward another stall.

We found her on her knees, under the display table. She was holding a long, orangish brown cattail—the marsh grass kind—that she had just pulled out of somebody's basket.

"Emmy!" Mom shrieked.

"I thought I found Silas," Emmy wailed. "I thought I saw *his* tail sticking up out of the basket."

She looked the way I feel when I strike out playing baseball.

"Don't cry, Emmy," I consoled. "It was a good try."

"Never mind," said Mom, giving her a hug.

"Come along now, gang," Dad was saying as he caught up to us. "We're going to get some lunch and have a picnic in Waterfront Park."

"Let's see if anybody's catching fish today," said Uncle Jim.

"Or anything else," Chad added.

E.

Waterfront Park

"Gol–ly!" What I saw when we entered the park surprised me. "That fountain looks like a giant pineapple." Silvery water sprayed out of it, making a splashing sound as it hit the pavement.

Behind us, downtown was already beginning to seem far away.

"I can't believe this," Dad exclaimed, as we started along the path crossing the lawn toward the Cooper River. We could see a boardwalk beside the river and a wharf where boats were tied and a long pier.

"It's taken years to build this beautiful, but neglected, site into a park," Uncle Jim explained. "We still call it a new park, although it opened in May 1990. We can all enjoy the riverfront here now."

"This was just a salt marsh when we were kids, wasn't it, Jim? Of course," my dad continued, "it was a busy place long, long ago when sailing ships took cargoes in and out of here."

"I'll beat you to the pier," Chad yelled.

"Don't run on the pier. Walk," instructed Uncle Jim.

"After you watch the fishermen for a few minutes, we'll eat lunch," Aunt Sue called.

Caroline, Emmy, and I were hurrying excitedly after Chad, out onto the pier. It was easy to see why we were not allowed to run. There was a deep drop over the sides, down to the water—*and* there were people sitting quietly holding fishing rods or standing and casting their lines who would not have liked our pounding past.

We watched as a boy about Emmy's size opened a bait box, took out a shrimp still in its shell, and fastened it onto the hook at the end of his line. A sunburned lady wearing a big straw hat showed him how to cast. The line flew out, and the bait hit the water and sank below the surface. We waited, but no fish seemed to be biting.

"Some days are luckier than others," the lady said. "Sometimes we catch sea trout and flounder here."

We heard Aunt Sue calling us to come and eat lunch, so we turned back.

Leaving the pier, we noticed an old man on the boardwalk carrying fish on a line hung over his shoulder. He seemed angry. He was yelling, "Scat. Scram. Beat it."

As we got closer, we could hear him muttering, "Blasted cat. Keeps trying to snitch all the fish I've caught."

Caroline and Chad and Emmy and I said in chorus, "**Cat? What cat?**"

"We didn't see a cat."

"What did he look like?"

"Where did he go?"

"Danged if I know," said the man. "He was here a minute ago. Glad he's gone, though. Big, orange cat, that's what he was."

The four of us looked all around, but there was no sign of that rascally Silas.

We bought hot dogs with everything on them—the works, just like in California—from a cart with a striped awning. Then we sat on benches under a shady tree and ate. Mom gave us some of the benne wafers and pralines—which we *don't* have for lunch in California. The benne wafers were little cookies made with sesame seeds. The pralines were big, flat candies made with nuts and brown sugar. They both tasted good!

Chad looked happy and content—and not just because of the lunch.

"I don't think he's following us," he said to me. "I think he's going ahead of us."

F.

The Old Exchange Building and Provost Dungeon

The next building we visited, just a short walk from the Cooper River, almost made me forget about Silas. It had a dungeon.

"This is the Old Exchange Building," Uncle Jim said, as we stood out front.

"Observe," Dad *lectured*, "the arched doorways and the handsome arched windows. This kind of architecture is called Palladian. The British built this place in 1770, when Charleston was still an English colony. It faced the busy harbor where ships without any power, except their sails, came and went from ports across the Atlantic Ocean and up and down the east coast."

"There was another building on this site almost a hundred years before this one," Uncle Jim added. "The earliest settlers had a village they called Charles Towne, instead of Charleston. It was small enough to have a wall around it to protect them from attacks by pirates or hostile Indians. Upstairs, here, was the town hall, and below was the dungeon where they kept prisoners."

"I want to tell the next part," Caroline said, as we went inside.

Sometimes she moved so fast she seemed to be almost dancing.

We entered two great adjoining halls that looked like ballrooms.

"George Washington visited here when the Revolution was over and South Carolina didn't belong to England any more," Caroline told us, "and the people of Charleston had a ball for him right in these rooms. Our his-

tory teacher told us about it. The ladies wore tall, white wigs with lots of curls and American flags stuck in them."

She was off twirling around again, as if she were at the ball, and Emmy twirled too—until some other tourists came in. Then they stopped and pretended they were just walking around the room's white pillars.

"Let's show David and Emmy the dungeon!" Chad was getting impatient.

It was great down there, kind of damp and dark and spooky. We had to walk under low brick arches that seemed older than anything we had seen before.

"Oh, my gosh!" I blurted.

There was a British officer standing right there, in his red coat, just inside the doorway and another English gentleman, probably the Provost, sitting at a desk. Of course, I knew they weren't real—after about a second, anyway—but the figures were *so* lifelike.

We ran around looking at all the other figures in the dungeon. There was a prisoner down on his knees, and another one with his hands in chains, and a supergruesome pirate with long, shaggy hair whose name was Stede Bonnet. Old Stede was one of the worst and most famous of them all, Chad said, and he was hanged at White Point Garden. He said a lot of other pirates were too. Their bodies were left hanging there for a long time to show what happened to criminals in Charles Towne.

While the rest of our family was looking at the skull and crossbones on the wall, where there was lots of other information about pirates, Chad and I sneaked behind the group and grabbed Caroline and Emmy.

"I am the ghost of Stede Bonnet!" Chad growled.

Emmy turned around. She had to show she wasn't fooled or scared. "Then I'm the ghost of Captain Hook," she snapped. Everybody laughed.

Suddenly, I stopped laughing. I thought I felt something warm and furry rub against my leg. I looked down, but in the dim light it was hard to be sure there was anything there. I looked at my sister and my cousins.

As we filed out of the dungeon one by one, I noticed that each of their faces seemed to have a look of surprise. I was pretty sure something *had* just scooted past us.

G.

Heyward-Washington House

"Why are all those houses painted pretty colors?" Emmy asked.

"That's a good question," Uncle Jim responded, as we walked along East Bay Street. "They've been painted blue and yellow and pink and green like that since long before I was born. We call that row of fourteen houses Rainbow Row. This section is one of the famous sights in Charleston."

We walked a few more blocks.

"I've been longing to see *inside* some of these beautiful old houses," my mom was saying.

Aunt Sue smiled. "Well, here's where you get your wish."

We stopped in front of a small brick house. There was a sign posted by the street and Caroline started reading it out loud.

"*During his visit to Charleston in 1791, as a guest of the people of Charleston, President George Washington was entertained in this house,*" she read. "He stayed right here when he went to that great ball. Can't you just imagine him coming out of this door and getting into a coach that would carry him right up these very same streets to that beautiful ballroom we just saw?"

Chad was getting that disgusted look he wore when he thought Caroline was showing off—but it *was* kind of awesome to imagine all that. I thought maybe she wasn't *really* showing off.

We went inside.

A lady took our tickets at the door and then started telling us about the place, called the Heyward-Washington House. It was owned by Tho-

25

mas Heyward, one of the South Carolina signers of the Declaration of Independence. It was built in 1772 and is a National Historic Landmark. As we walked through the rooms, the guide told us about the china and the furniture and everything, but Chad and I were only halfway listening.

"Do you think a cat could sneak in here when nobody is looking?" Chad asked me quietly.

"I don't know. Maybe," I whispered back.

We lagged behind the other visitors and checked things out as we went along.

I started paying attention again in a bedroom upstairs where the shaving stand George Washington used sat beside a fireplace. It was funny to think of George Washington shaving right there beside that fireplace and then putting on the white wig he was wearing in the picture downstairs.

Mom was admiring the four-poster bed that had a short, little curtain thing, called a canopy, all around the top. The guide pointed out the carvings of acanthus leaves on the posts.

"I hope," she said politely but sternly, "that no one has been sitting on the bed."

Everybody looked. There was a hollowed-out place on the pillow— just the right size for a curled-up cat.

The lady plumped up the pillow. "Strange," she mumbled quietly to herself, "that spot felt a little warm. . . . Oh, well," she said to the group, "let's move on. I'm sure that wasn't the fault of anybody here."

We kids all grinned at each other but didn't say anything.

The guide led us downstairs and out the back door, through a little garden, to the restored kitchen. Long ago they cooked over a huge fireplace in that building. There were all kinds of funny, old-fashioned cooking gadgets to see.

"There's supposed to be a secret wine closet here," Dad said. "Can any of you kids guess where it is?"

We all guessed, but the guide finally had to show us. . . . *I know now*

where it is, of course, but I'm not telling. . . .

We went last to the washhouse, where the laundry was done in water heated in another big fireplace. I had fun pretending I was going to put Emmy in the big oval washtub, and she had fun ducking away from me.

"We'd better leave," Mom said as she moved toward the door.

"We'll catch your rascally cat at the next stop," I said quietly to my cousins. "He must have had a *very* short nap."

H.

Nathaniel Russell House

"Are you children getting tired?" Aunt Sue asked.

"No, we're not tired," answered Chad. "Are we?" he asked looking at Caroline, Emmy, and me.

"No, we're not tired," we all said together.

Pointing toward the steps, my mom said, "Let's go in, then,"

Uncle Jim looked at us and winked. "Who knows what we might find in there?"

"Don't encourage them, Jim," Aunt Sue scolded. "You know they're just playing a game about that cat."

We had stopped in front of a house that stood back from the street behind a fancy fence. It looked just like a picture in a history book.

"Observe," said Dad, "the elliptical center of the building. That means it's curved out. This mansion is a great example of the architectural style called Federal. It was built by Nathaniel Russell in 1808."

We went into the garden first. "Oh, these Charleston gardens!" Mom exclaimed. . . . I think she had run out of words like charming and lovely and beautiful.

Then, we went inside the house. After giving our tickets to the attendant at the door, Dad just stood there with his hands on his hips looking at the stairway leading from the hall. It curved around and up, three stories high.

"Why do you think this is called the 'flying staircase'?" he asked us.

"Because it looks like it's flying?" That was Emmy.

"Because there's nothing holding it up?" I asked.

"Both right. It's an architectural triumph," Dad said. "All by itself, it soars."

"Observe," said our lady guide—and we giggled because she sounded just like Dad—"the ornamental plaster mouldings and . . . ." Well, she went on to explain about things like that and about how the furniture was all made at the same time that Nathaniel Russell lived in the house. When we peeked into the dining room, Caroline whispered that it was just as well Silas wasn't prowling around in there with all the glass and silver and china painted with pictures of fruit on the long table. Sometimes he bumped things, she said, and wouldn't that be **awful**?

We went up the flying stairs and passed a large window that made the whole house seem kind of light and airy. We kids followed the group to a room our guide called the drawing room and then down a short hall to the music room. We stopped to stare at a golden harp, taller than Caroline. She reached up and pretended she was playing the strings.

The grown-ups moved on to the old-fashioned bedrooms. The music room seemed empty now and very quiet. While the others were looking at the canopied beds and stuff, we started for the stairs again. That flying staircase was fun!

That's when we heard the sounds.

Somebody was playing the harp. . . . Well, not really *playing*. Something was touching the strings so that we heard little pings, starting low and then going higher—*ping, ping, ping, ping, ping* up and then *ping, ping, ping, ping, ping* down again.

We crept back upstairs.

There was no one in the music room where the golden harp stood. The last string, as if it had been touched, made one faint *ping*.

We almost flew down the flying staircase. The back door was open. The ticket lady had gone outside and was talking with some people who were leaving.

All we saw was the flick of an orange tail, disappearing around a lower corner of the doorway.

I.

The Battery and White Point Garden

"I could have grabbed that slippery little critter," Chad moaned, "if we'd been one minute faster. Now he'll be ahead of us again."

"I just hope he doesn't get into trouble." Caroline was still worried.

"Relax." Uncle Jim had just reached the door and heard Caroline's remark. "I'm going home now to get the van. We have to drive to see the last place—the surprise we were telling you about. I'll bet Silas is right there at home on his blanket. Now," he continued, turning to the other parents, "why don't you take the kids down Water Street to the Battery? You can wait for me there."

We walked right down to the tip of Charleston and reached a park with grass and trees and benches, called White Point Garden—where the pirates were hanged—and a seawall that looked as if it was holding the land in, keeping it from the water that swished around it. There were old cannons placed in a line along the seawall. These were used to guard the city, Dad said, in the old days. That's why the area is called the Battery. . . . Those old cannons look as if they're still guarding the city.

"You can see now that this city was built on a peninsula," Dad said.

"What's a peninsula?" asked Emmy.

"A point of land, like a finger. Look here on our left side. That's the Cooper River. On the right side is the Ashley River. Charleston was built on the land between the two rivers, although it's not cut off all around as an island is. The rivers come together and make a harbor. Then they both

32

flow into the sea. Out there," he said, pointing, "is the Atlantic Ocean."

"Gosh," I said. I had seen only one other ocean, the Pacific.

Mom must have guessed what I was thinking.

"So here we are, all the way from California," she said. "From sea to shining sea."

"That's from a song, isn't it? . . . *America the Beautiful?*" Caroline asked Mom. . . . *As if we didn't know!* . . .

"If you glance behind you," Aunt Sue said, "you'll see a famous Charleston scene. Those elegant houses lined up along East Battery and South Battery have been there looking out to sea for a long, long time."

"And if you look ahead, you'll see Fort Sumter on that little island, way out at the entrance to the harbor," Dad added. "That might be the most famous sight of all. The Confederate soldiers fired the first cannon shot of the War Between the States at that fort in 1861, because the northern army occupied it."

"It's neat out there," said Chad. "You can go inside the walls of the old fort, and park rangers tell you how it guarded the harbor and how the Confederates got it back and stayed there until it was almost demolished. 'Course, the North did win the war, but not Fort Sumter."

Emmy was getting tired of history. "Let's go climb a cannon," she said.

Chad and I raced her to the nearest one.

We were just about to become the Confederate army defending the city again, when we heard a horn honking and saw Uncle Jim motioning to us, so we hurried to the van.

"Was Silas home?" asked Chad, as we all climbed in.

"Well . . . no," Uncle Jim answered, "he wasn't, but I'm sure he'll be there when we get back."

J.
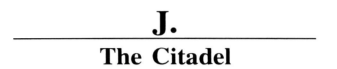
The Citadel

Uncle Jim wouldn't tell us where we were going. He said we'd have to see it first.

After a short drive, we arrived at a place that looked like a huge white fort, with castle turrets on one end.

"This is The Citadel," he explained, "the military school of South Carolina where young people can go to college and also learn to be officers in any branch of military service. Caroline and Chad love to come on Friday afternoons when school is in session to see the cadets in their dress parade, so we thought you California kids would like it too."

"The dress parade is neat," Chad said. "The band plays and a cannon goes boom, and the cadets come marching out in formation."

"They have to be perfect," Caroline chimed in. "They all march in step and they look straight ahead until they come to the place where the commanding officer stands. Then they all turn their heads at the same time and . . . well, you'll see."

I was excited as we walked through the open iron gates. I could already hear a band playing.

Inside, the parade ground was bigger than a football field. It was shaped like a square, surrounded by all the Citadel buildings. My cousins pointed out the classroom building, the chapel, and the barracks. There were bleachers and paths and shady trees bordering the field. Lots of people were standing around. Many were already seated in the bleachers, waiting for the parade to begin.

"Hey, look," I said, pointing. There was a real airplane parked on one side of the field and a real army tank not far from that.

"Can we climb in 'em?" I wanted to know.

"Better not now." Aunt Sue checked her watch. "It's almost 3:45. That's when the parade starts and everything here has to move with military precision." She glanced down at Emmy. "That means *exactly right*."

"Look, David, there's the mascot." Chad pointed.

Off on the edge of the field, near the place where we had stood just a few minutes before, two tall boys were holding the leash on a big bulldog.

"They don't usually have the mascot at dress parades, do they?" Dad asked.

"No, only at sports events," Uncle Jim answered. "Maybe he's just being exercised."

That big old bulldog just sat there looking tough, the way bulldogs do.

"Boy, he's a great mascot," I said. "He looks as if he's thinking, 'You'd better not mess with me.'"

The band started playing again and out from under an archway marched the cadets in formation. They looked really cool in their blue-gray coats and spanking clean white pants. Their feet made thuds on the grass all at the same time.

The two flag bearers in front looked very proud, carrying our "red, white, and blue" on the right and the state flag on the left. I began thinking that maybe I'd like to come to The Citadel some day.

"The whole group is called a regiment," Caroline whispered to me. "They march in long rows like that, divided into companies."

The companies kept passing by us—left, right, left, right—but in spite of the sound of marching feet and music from the band, which was making me feel like marching too, I thought I heard something, sort of a low, fierce growl.

Chad punched me.

While everybody else was watching the dress parade, he was watching

the bulldog.

The mascot was pulling against the leash, and—*yes*—he was growling at something he saw, or smelled, that bothered him.

Just then, right in front of the bulldog, we saw something move so fast it looked like an orange streak. In another second, the dog was loose and after it.

"Silas!" yelled Chad.

The two cadets started racing after their mascot. Chad started running after the cadets. Caroline saw what was happening and sprinted into the chase to save Silas. I ran after Caroline. Emmy ran after me.

The bulldog ran right through the last row of the formation. The cadets looked straight ahead and kept on marching.

"Come on!" panted Chad. "We can't let him catch Silas!"

All of a sudden that big old bulldog plopped down on the other side of the field. Whatever he was chasing was gone.

Everything happened so fast—and we were running too fast to stop. The two cadets bumped into the bulldog. Chad bumped into the cadets. Caroline bumped into Chad. I bumped into Caroline. Emmy bumped into the last cadet in the last row of the formation. We all fell over and sat upright on the grass.

The cadet who was in formation was up in a flash and marching in step as his company turned a corner of the field.

"Whew!" sighed one of the fallen cadets. He grabbed the mascot's collar and refastened the leash. "I bet we'll never do this again."

Our parents were waving to us to come back to their side of the field. They didn't look too happy.

"You kids could have disrupted the whole parade," my dad said.

"It's a good thing the commotion occurred in the back of the formation," Uncle Jim remarked. "I don't think many people saw what was going on."

"I couldn't tell just what was happening," my mom said, "but I noticed that last cadet was having some kind of problem. He was looking straight ahead, but he seemed to be either choking or trying not to laugh. And why did he have grass stains on his nice, white pants?"

• • • • • • • • • •

That night, Aunt Sue said we should get to bed soon after dinner because we'd need an early start the next day.

By half past nine, Silas still had not come home.

Chad put a dish of cat food by the door on the piazza, and Caroline placed a bowl of milk right beside it.

"Silas loves milk," she said. "He thinks he's a very tough cat, but sometimes he acts like a baby. Maybe he'll be hungry and tired and go right to sleep after he has his supper."

Then Caroline went off to her room for the night.

My mom and dad were sleeping in Chad's room. Emmy was sharing Caroline's room. Chad and I were the luckiest. We crawled into sleeping bags in the den.

"I think I have a plan," Chad said.

"Great." Chad always had a plan. "What's going to happen tomorrow?" I asked.

"Settle down, kids," Dad called down. "Absolutely no more talking."

Aunt Sue was turning off the lights.

"Tomorrow," she said, "we're going to see three low country plantations."

"What's a low country plantation?" Emmy's sleepy voice drifted from Caroline's room.

"You can hear all about it in the morning." Mom's voice sounded sleepy too.

"**Good night!**" Dad said. He sounded as if he meant it.

K.
Middleton Place

In the morning, the cat food and milk were still sitting by the door, but Silas was nowhere to be found.

Chad and Caroline were busy making signs that read MISSING CAT: ORANGE, FIVE TOES ON EACH PAW. They wrote the address on Tradd Street across the bottom.

"Come along, now," said Uncle Jim. "It's time to leave. You know, Silas isn't only an athletic cat, he's an explorer. You might call him the Marco Polo of the cat world. He often stays away for a day or two, but he knows where his home is. So, let's not worry about him today. If he's not here when we get back, we'll all help you put your signs around the neighborhood."

Our parents walked toward the van.

As we kids crowded into the back seats, Chad looked at me and patted his bulgy jacket pocket. I knew he had a can of milk and a little dish in there. The plan was simple. If we had any clue, anywhere, that Silas was around, Chad would put the dish down quickly and fill it with milk. Silas would make a dash for the milk—my cousins were sure of that—and, while he was lapping it up, *maybe* we could catch him.

As we crossed the bridge over the Ashley River, heading away from downtown, Dad said, "I guess it's time for us old Charlestonians to tell Emmy and David about low country plantations."

"Well, gosh, Dad, anybody can see that the land here is low," I said. "It's not much higher than the rivers are."

"Well, gosh, Dad," said Emmy—as if she hadn't asked about this the night before—"anybody would know that on plantations they *planted* things."

Dad smiled. "Good thinking," he said. "So what do you think those early landowners, who had acres and acres of this gentle low country, planted?"

I had to think about that one. "Cotton?" I guessed.

"Yes, and indigo, a plant that was used to dye things blue. But they weren't the only crops. The other one was—"

"Rice," said Caroline and Chad together.

I made a sort of circle with my hands above my head. "Light bulb," I said. "I remember some pictures in my geography book of people standing in water, planting rice, but I thought that was only in places like China."

"It was quite a science," Dad responded. "The rice was raised here on these and other plantations in separated fields that were flooded at high tide and drained at low tide by a system of canals and little dams. It's not practical to do this here anymore, but a lot of the money that paid for the three gorgeous places you're going to see today came from those fields of rice."

"We're going to Middleton Place, Magnolia Gardens, and Drayton Hall," Aunt Sue said. "There'll be different things in each place that you children will have fun seeing and hearing about. Of course, no one lives in these beautiful old houses now, and the land isn't farmed as it used to be, but the plantations are kept open to the public so everyone can enjoy them and imagine a time in our American history that's gone forever."

By this time we were riding along a winding road with woods on either side.

"This is the Ashley River Road," Uncle Jim said. "It's one of the oldest highways in the United States. And now, it's time for you kids to start using your imaginations. We are not driving down this road in a car; we are arriving in a carriage."

"Oh, Dad," Chad groaned—but I think he was just trying to be cool

"We're coming to see the Middleton family," Aunt Sue added, smiling.

"And we're terribly sorry about their house," said Caroline, "because it was burned during the War Between the States, and then, soon after that, it was totalled by an earthquake."

"Well, not all of it," Chad corrected her. "See?"

We were driving through an open gate and down a lane beside a long stretch of green grass where sheep were nibbling. At the far end was a red brick house with three tall chimneys, surrounded by a low brick wall.

When we went inside the house, the lady tour guide told our group that this was only part of the original house, the right side, which had once been the wing where gentleman guests stayed. When this wing was all that was left of the house, the whole family lived there.

She told us about the first Henry Middleton, who came to live on the plantation when the house was a mansion, years and years ago—like more than two hundred—and started planning the gardens and ponds and lakes. Henry's son Arthur was one of the signers of the Declaration of Independence. . . . And the story went on that way, like part of a history book.

Chad, who had heard all this before, kept getting close to me, patting his pocket.

Caroline and Emmy hung back with us, as the group of visitors moved forward through the house. The Middleton house is called a museum now, and my mom was having a great time looking at the collections of pictures, books, silver, and stuff.

"Do you really think Silas could still be following us?" Caroline whispered.

"Or going ahead of us?" I whispered too. "It's a long way, Chad."

"Just keep checking," Chad said. "Let's be ready. As soon as we're through the house, we'll go to the stable yards. They're lots of animals around that place."

We could hardly wait to get outside, although it was sort of fun to see the room upstairs where all the old toys were.

As we walked out of the house, Chad said, "Now let's go to the stable yards, Dad."

"Oh, but you don't want to miss the elegant formal gardens," said Aunt Sue. "The azaleas are all in bloom. And just look—those are the famous Butterfly Lakes."

She pointed to a place beyond the house where the lawn rolled down and down and down in steps to a pair of lakes that did, in fact, look like a butterfly's wings. Below the lakes was the Ashley River.

If a person started rolling . . . . "Wouldn't it be fun to—" I started to say.

"Don't even think about it!" Uncle Jim was quick to interrupt my thought. "Look," he said to the other grown-ups, "I'll take the kids around to the stables while you enjoy the gardens."

We all yelled, "Yea!"

We went first to the rice mill pond and climbed down the steps into the dark little underground spring house. That was fun, but we didn't see any signs of a large orange cat. Then, finally, we went to the stable yards. I could see right away that's where the action was.

The area reminded me of movies I'd seen of olden days on a country farm, except everything here was real. There were real farm animals—horses and cows and mules and goats, and guinea hens that looked like weird chickens. There was a long, low building sectioned into different workrooms, and in each small room a craftsperson showed how a particular job was done on the plantation.

As we walked, Uncle Jim explained that, in the early days, the main road to these plantations along the Ashley River was really not a road at all but the river itself. It took a long time for supplies to reach the docks of each place because they had to come from across the sea. So each plantation had to grow or make most of what was needed to take care of the people who lived there. Many of the slaves who did the work—in the days before all slaves were made free—had special jobs, like spinning yarn for cloth or grinding corn or making horseshoes.

We watched a potter making a jug out of clay, and we saw a spinning wheel and a loom where they wove clothes out of hanks of wool that had come from their own sheep.

The blacksmith was making horseshoes, so we stopped at his shed. He put pieces of iron into a smokey old stone fireplace and left them there until they were red as cherries. Then he took them out with long tongs and beat them on an anvil into the shape of a horse's foot.

I was watching him put a horseshoe into a tub of cold water and listening for it to sizzle, when back in one of the dark corners I heard a faint *mewing*.

My cousins heard it too.

That was the only clue Chad needed.

In a flash, he had that can of milk out of his pocket and opened, and had a dish of milk on the floor. We backed off and waited, so quiet we were barely breathing.

Then out from the shadows came a little black cat. She ran right over to the dish and began drinking the milk.

Chad just stood there, looking so surprised Caroline and Emmy and I started laughing. After awhile, Chad joined in and then we couldn't stop. We were kind of whooping and choking, and the blacksmith stopped working to find out what was so funny.

"You see," Chad tried to explain, "we were trying to catch our own cat."

"We can't find him," I said.

"He loves milk," Caroline told the man. "And we were sure we heard Silas. But that little black cat—"

"Came and drank it all up," said Emmy.

The blacksmith looked thoughtful.

"Is your cat—Silas—kind of a reddish yellow color?"

"Yes!" All four of us answered together.

"Kind of a *big* cat?"

"Yes!"

"Well, kids, there was a cat like that here just a little while ago—at milking time. Thomas had hardly finished milking the cow, set the pail to one side, and turned his head, when that cat came speeding out of nowhere and got himself a nice long drink."

"Where did he go?" Chad and Caroline were both looking all around.

"I'm sorry, kids, but I couldn't say. He just took off. He looked kind of tuckered out."

"Don't get your hopes up, gang." Uncle Jim walked up behind us. "That cat might not have been Silas."

But our hopes were already up.

"We'll catch him at the next place," said Chad. "He must be getting tired."

L.
Magnolia Plantation and Gardens

Aunt Sue was telling us that many people who know all about gardens believe that the gardens of Magnolia Plantation are the most beautiful in the world, but I was more interested in the strange little animals in the field along the driveway.

"What are those—over there?" I didn't exactly interrupt. I just plunged in when Aunt Sue ran out of breath. "They look like horses, but they're much too small."

"They are horses—miniatures—a rare and special breed," Uncle Jim explained. "You can take a closer look at them a little later because they're near the Petting Zoo."

"Oh, they look so *cute*. They aren't even as tall as I am. Can we pet them? Can we pet other animals too?" Emmy was excited.

"You may be able to stroke the minihorses if they come over to the fence," Aunt Sue said, "but in the Petting Zoo you can touch the animals easily—and feed them. People are even allowed to bring their own animals here, if they have them on leashes."

"I wish we had Silas on a leash," Caroline sighed.

"No way!" Chad said. "He's a very proud cat."

We were all laughing at the thought of Silas on a leash as we piled out of the van and started toward the house and the Orientation Theater.

"The house looks interesting," Mom said, "but it doesn't seem to be as old as the wing of the house we just saw at Middleton Plantation."

"It isn't," Dad said. "The original Magnolia Plantation house was burned too."

"This house," said Aunt Sue, "was once used as a country retreat in a town called Summerville, about ten miles away, on the Ashley River. It was brought, piece by piece, down the river after the War Between the States. It's furnished in the style of the Victorian period, just as it was when the family lived here."

I had a hard time trying to imagine how they moved the house. That was a big house, although it wasn't a mansion, and pretty old. And it had a tower on the top with windows in it. All I could picture in my mind was that tower sailing down the Ashley River.

Dad was leading us toward the Orientation Theater.

"The Draytons have lived here for ten generations," he said. "When we see the film, we'll understand more about the history of the plantation."

When we came out of the theater, Uncle Jim volunteered to take us kids on the garden walking tour that led to the Wildlife Observation Tower. We passed the herb garden and the garden where all the plants are the same as the ones told about in the Bible. We walked past bushes so tall they almost seemed like trees with flowers on them. We followed the path along the river. Flowers were blooming everywhere.

"Don't forget," Uncle Jim said, "long ago, somebody planted these, although they look as if they just began growing here by themselves. There are more than nine hundred kinds of camellias."

The camellias he showed us were really pretty, but I was beginning to think we might have to see all nine hundred kinds, when Chad said, "Look, there's the observation tower."

It was awesome. We climbed up to a platform fifty feet high. Standing up there, we could see the river bordering the plantation, and, directly below, a blue lake with brown marsh grass around it. Flocks of tall white birds that Uncle Jim called egrets stalked in the water.

"If you watch closely, you may see some wild geese or a great blue heron or a bald eagle or an alligator or a red-winged blackbird," he told us.

We did see a big old turtle, moving slowly under the surface of the water, some wild ducks—mallards—with shiny green heads, and then we were pretty sure we saw an alligator. We all thought about Silas.

"This would not be a good place for a tired cat," said Caroline.

We hurried to the Pavilion, where we were meeting the rest of the family for lunch.

The Pavilion was near the Petting Zoo, so after we ate, we went to see the animals. Mom bought us corn to feed them and we went inside the fence. It was fun—and so different from the Wildlife Sanctuary, where you really sort of *spy* on wild creatures. In the Petting Zoo the animals were tame and gentle. There were baby goats and bunnies and a lamb and, best of all, a little deer, a fawn like Bambi. There were peacocks too, wandering around, spreading their tails into big fans, sometimes making funny sounds like babies crying. We didn't try to feed or touch the peacocks.

Emmy still wanted to see the little horses. They were near the zoo in their own pasture. As we started toward them, something happened behind us—something that disturbed the peacocks. There was superloud *crying*. Those peacocks sounded pitiful, but mad. We turned around. Three of those big birds, that usually don't seem to fly very much, were perched on top of the wire fence.

We all said the same thing—even the grown-ups, who knew what we were thinking—"Silas!"

"Come on, Blakes," said Uncle Jim, laughing, "let's not get carried away. Now, we'll see the horses, and then, before we leave Magnolia, I have something amazing to show you."

"Oh, Dad," Caroline and Chad groaned, but they wouldn't tell us what he meant.

When we found out, even Mom and Dad said, "Oh, Jim."

"Well, it is amazing," Uncle Jim said, grinning, as he led us into the maze.

A maze is a giant puzzle. You walk through narrow paths between high hedges and try to find your way out.

"This one," Aunt Sue told us as we walked, "was copied from a famous maze in the Hampton Court Palace gardens in England."

It didn't take long for us to get to the middle. There was a statue there and four benches, where we sat to rest a minute.

"Now let's see who can find the way out," Dad said.

It seemed easy at first, but then, just as you thought you were on the right path, you'd come to a dead end and have to go back. Our parents had let us four cousins go ahead and we didn't want to admit we were lost. Even Chad and Caroline couldn't remember which way to go.

"I think . . . this way," I said, turning to a path on the left. I was only guessing. I looked down at the roots of the hedge along the path to see if I could see through, but I couldn't. What I did see, under the hedge just ahead of us, was an orange tail.

I stood very still and pointed. Caroline, Emmy, and Chad looked toward the hedge. The tail didn't move.

"I told you he's getting tired," Chad whispered. "If Silas is under there, he's asleep."

We moved forward carefully. We were almost close enough to grab him, and the tail disappeared. We kept sneaking forward. The tail appeared again, around the corner. We sneaked closer. The tail disappeared. We continued to creep along and it appeared again. When we got close, it was gone.

"Congratulations," our parents called behind us. We were out!

We looked all around, but we didn't see the cat that went with the orange tail.

"All you had to do," Uncle Jim said, "was keep turning to the left, but I didn't think you kids should try it without a grown-up."

"We were just lucky, I guess," Chad said.

"That wasn't luck," Caroline whispered. "I think Silas led us out."

"I think so too," Chad agreed, "but I don't think the grown-ups would believe us."

M.
Drayton Hall Plantation

Uncle Jim was telling us about Hurricane Hugo as we turned in at the entrance to Drayton Hall, the plantation that sits next door to Magnolia.

He explained that the road to the house is called an avenue, and that it was like a green tunnel, with branches of giant trees almost meeting overhead, before Hugo roared through Charleston. Many trees crashed during the storm and had to be sawed up and taken away.

"Get ready, kids, we're going to play a game called *observation*," my dad said.

We all looked at each other and laughed, but we got ready.

"Now," Dad went on, "the first person to see the house has to call out a one-word description of it, the first thing that pops into your head."

We all saw it at the same time.

I yelled "Big" while Chad yelled "Old" and Emmy yelled "Beautiful." Wouldn't you know Caroline showed off with "Symmetrical"?

Caroline and Chad had been to Drayton Hall lots of times before, for education programs. The one that sounded the most fun to me was when they learned about archaeology and even got to dig for artifacts.

After we parked the van and turned in our tickets, we walked toward the house and sat on the Charleston benches where the tour would begin. While we sat waiting, everybody was very, very quiet. There was something about that great, big, old house, sitting in the middle of the gigantic green lawn, that was truly awesome. For a few minutes, I think even Chad and Caroline forgot about Silas.

At the beginning of the tour, the guide told us a lot about the Drayton family and the reasons why the house is so special. My dad was smiling and nodding at everything, especially when the guide said, "Drayton Hall is considered to be one of the first and finest examples of Georgian-Palladian architecture in this country. It was built for young John Drayton in 1738, when George Washington was only six years old."

I was imagining all the kids who lived in this house since the first Draytons moved in. After the War Between the States, we were told, they mostly lived downtown in Charleston, but they loved to come out here to the country where it was much more fun. I'll bet it was neat to travel back and forth on the Ashley River, instead of in a car.

Walking into the house was like *being* in history, instead of just hearing about it—because the house hasn't changed much since it was built. The guide said that was another reason the place is so special. It has been preserved, which means kept the same as it was, rather than restored, which means put back to look the way it was.

Soldiers camped on the property during the Revolutionary War, but didn't damage the house. During the Civil War most of the other plantation houses along the Ashley River were burned, but not Drayton Hall. It also stayed strong and sound through a terrible earthquake in 1886, and even through Hurricane Hugo in 1989.

A great word I could have used in Dad's observation game popped into my mind: **invincible**. But I didn't tell anybody because we were already moving through the house.

There were lots of tours going on in the house the same time as ours. We heard one group speaking a foreign language. Aunt Sue said it was French. Their guide had to wait for the interpreter to repeat everything that was said, so they were moving pretty slowly.

Our group had to go a different way, so we wouldn't keep bumping into the other tours, but we were the last group—and, finally, the *only* group left in the house.

My mom had run out of words again when we looked up at the plaster ceilings in the drawing room. It had vines and flowers, and right in the center were ears of corn. Dad said the wood carvings on the other mouldings, which were everywhere, were some of the best he had ever seen. It was easy to find "egg and dart" and "dentil" moulding, because they looked just like what they were called.

Emmy said the room she liked best was the one where lots of Drayton kids had their height measured and marked on one side of the door frame. On the other side of the door, Miss Charlotta Drayton measured four of her dogs. Chad told us that her favorite dog, Nipper, was buried on the grounds outside, and the grave even has a real headstone. He promised to show it to us after the tour.

Our guide said we shouldn't miss the small yellow room, the only one we hadn't seen, because there was something special in there that children in particular enjoyed—real mouseholes in the baseboard, like in a *Tom and Jerry* cartoon.

The guide pushed open the creaky door, then stopped and stared, just as surprised at the sight as the rest of us.

There, lying in a patch of warm afternoon sunlight, right next to the two mouseholes, was a big, beautiful, gorgeous, but kind of bedraggled, orange cat. When he saw us, he stood up slowly, arching his back in a lazy stretch that went right down to his *five* toes. Of course, it was Silas, giving us a look that said, "Well, it's about time you caught up with me!"

• • • • • • • • • •

On the way home, in the van, Silas was content to let Caroline and Chad take turns holding him. He seemed very tired.

"We knew it," said Chad. "We knew Silas was coming with us, as soon as David and I saw his paw prints on that garden wall!"

David turned one of Silas's paws out gently and I could see the five

little toes. But, Silas pulled his paw back, away from me, and looked disdainful before he snuggled down again. He was tired but he was still a very proud cat.

"I knew it!" Emmy chimed in excitedly. "I knew it as soon as we saw his tail sliding along the railing above that clock in the church tower."

"We were sure he was going ahead of us, remember," Caroline asked, "when that man in the park told us a big orange cat had been trying to steal his fish?"

"Now, children," said Aunt Sue, "you're letting your imaginations run away with you. Somebody must have seen that poor cat dragging along the road somewhere and picked him up in a car and then let him out again, somewhere close to Drayton Hall."

"But, Mom," Caroline said, leaning forward, "Silas was right in front of those two little old mouseholes. Do you think he knew they were there?"

Chad and I were thinking the same thing, so we said it at the same time, "**Maybe cats do have nine lives.**"

Caroline spoke slowly, as if she was solving a puzzle, "Maybe Silas really was our tour guide, showing us some of the favorite places he lived in some of his other lives."

Dad turned around and grinned at us, and at that moment he didn't look much like a grown-up himself. Then he turned back and looked at Uncle Jim. "I don't know, Jim," he said. "What do you think?"

"Well," said Uncle Jim, "Silas *is* a very athletic cat. How would you rate him as a tour guide, kids, on a scale of one to ten?"

We didn't even have to think about it. Together, with all our might, we yelled, "**TEN!**"

The End

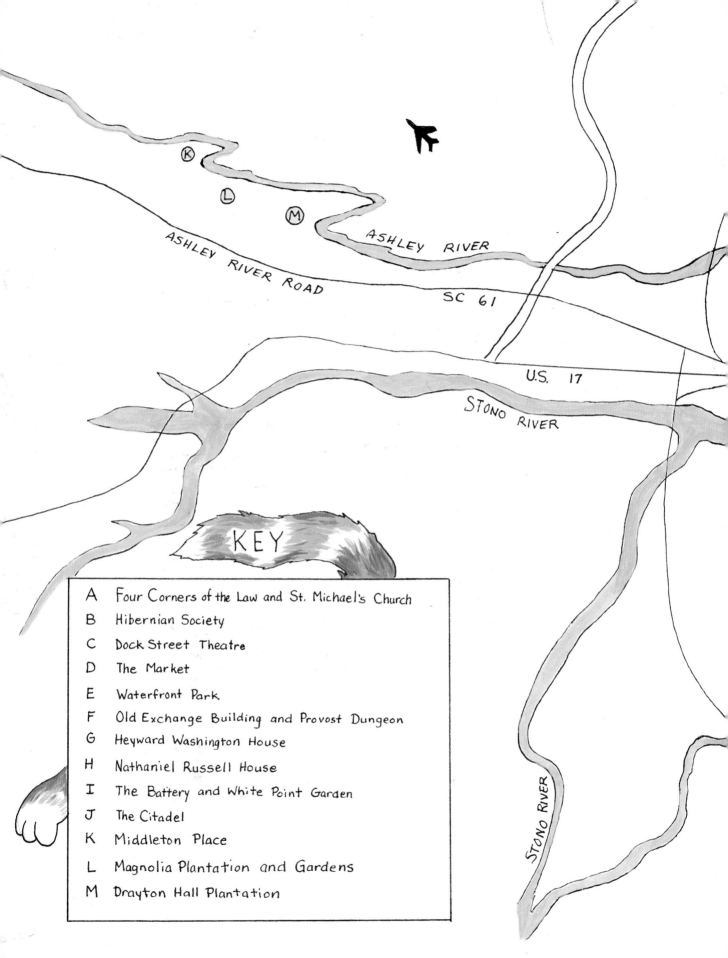

KEY

A	Four Corners of the Law and St. Michael's Church
B	Hibernian Society
C	Dock Street Theatre
D	The Market
E	Waterfront Park
F	Old Exchange Building and Provost Dungeon
G	Heyward Washington House
H	Nathaniel Russell House
I	The Battery and White Point Garden
J	The Citadel
K	Middleton Place
L	Magnolia Plantation and Gardens
M	Drayton Hall Plantation

ASHLEY RIVER ROAD

ASHLEY RIVER

SC 61

U.S. 17

STONO RIVER

STONO RIVER

About the authors:

RUTH ("Booie") PATERSON CHAPPELL is on the education staff at Drayton Hall Plantation, having taught school prior to moving to Charleston. Booie received her BA in early childhood education from the University of Maryland and continued her graduate work at Towson State. She is a member of the Charleston Alumnae Association of Kappa Kappa Gamma, the South Carolina Historical Society, the Preservation Society of Charleston, and the National Trust for Historic Preservation.

Booie and her husband Chris live on Drayton Hall Plantation. They enjoy the companionship of their eleven-year-old black Labrador Retriever, Nick, and the frequent visits of their children and grandchildren.

BESS PATERSON SHIPE is a freelance writer. She received her BA in English from the University of Maryland and has continued her study with courses in novel and freelance writing. She was an English teacher in the Baltimore County school system before marrying and learning more about children firsthand. Bess is a member of the Washington Independent Writers and the Washington-Suburban Alumnae Association of Kappa Kappa Gamma. She is active in her local book club and enjoys historic research, gardening, and visits with her five grandchildren.

Bess and her husband Kelso make their home in Potomac, Maryland, just minutes from the Potomac River.

About the illustrator:

DEAN GRAY WROTH is a freelance artist. She received a BA in fine art from Marietta College (Ohio) and is an active member of her local fine arts league. She previously served as arts/crafts supervisor with the Montgomery County (MD) Department of Recreation. Her interests include gardening, cooking, classical music, and ballet.

Dean and her husband Ted share a home with their two daughters, Sarah and Mary Kate, in Poolesville, Maryland.